Julia Donaldson

Yuval Zommer

The WOOLLY BEAR CATERPILLAR

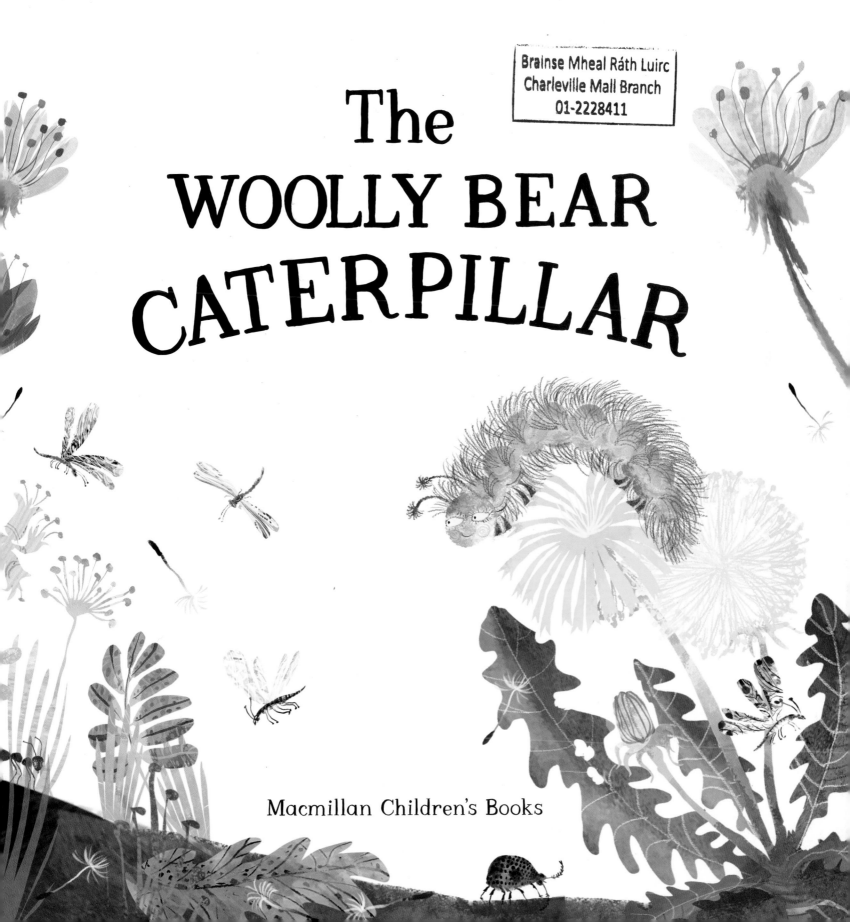

Macmillan Children's Books

There was once a woolly bear caterpillar. She lived in a garden and she loved eating dandelion leaves.

But one day, a gardener
pulled up all the dandelions
in the flower bed.

The woolly bear caterpillar had to
crawl off in search of some new ones.

She hadn't crawled far when she heard someone singing. On a leaf of a sycamore tree sat a caterpillar with very long yellow and orange hair, and this was her song . . .

"Look at me!
Look at me!
I'm bonny and bright as can be.
With my hair of bright gold,
I'm a joy to behold,
The queen of the sycamore tree."

"Hello. What's your name?" asked the woolly bear caterpillar. "I'm a sycamore caterpillar, and I'm going to turn into a sycamore moth. Just think — if I'm so pretty now, I'll be absolutely gorgeous when I get my wings."

"I'm going to have wings too one day," said the woolly bear caterpillar.

The sycamore caterpillar laughed.
"Yes, very plain ones, I expect.
Never mind, we can't all be beautiful."

The woolly bear caterpillar crawled
on till she reached an apple tree.
On a fallen apple sat a caterpillar with
red spots and bright yellow tufts.
He was singing this song . . .

"Look at me!
Look at me!
I'm snazzy and smart as can be.
With my tufts of bright yellow,
    I'm such a fine fellow,
The king of the old apple tree."

"Hello. What's your name?" asked the woolly bear caterpillar.
"I'm a vapourer caterpillar. I'm good-looking, aren't I?
And I'll be even more handsome when I'm a moth."

"I'll be a moth too one day,"
said the woolly bear caterpillar.

The vapourer caterpillar laughed.
"Yes, a very dull one, I imagine.
Never mind, we can't all be colourful."

The woolly bear caterpillar crawled on till she came to a tall poplar tree. On a twig was a very strange-looking caterpillar.

He was bright green, and round his head were some red marks that made it look as if he was screaming. He was singing this song . . .

"Look at me!
Look at me!
I'm stunning and strange as can be.
The marks round my head
Are a fierce fiery red.
I'm the king of the tall poplar tree."

"Hello. What's your name?" asked the woolly bear caterpillar. "I'm a puss moth caterpillar. Don't I look weird and wonderful? And if I'm so unusual now, just think how extraordinary I'll be when I become a moth."

"I wonder what sort of moth I'll become," said the woolly bear caterpillar.

The puss moth caterpillar laughed.
"A very boring one, I should think," he said.
"Never mind, we can't all be perfect."

The woolly bear caterpillar felt a little sad.
She wished she could be beautiful and exciting
instead of plain and dull. But then at last she
found some dandelion leaves, which cheered her up.

After a tasty meal, she
crawled under a big dock leaf.
"It's time I got ready to change
into a moth," she decided, and
she started to spin herself a
nice silky coat called a cocoon.

The sycamore caterpillar was spinning a cocoon too, in some old leaves on the ground.

The vapourer caterpillar's
cocoon was on a twig
of the apple tree.

And the puss moth caterpillar
had found a snug hole in the
poplar tree's bark for his cocoon.

Weeks went by. Then
it was time for the
moths to hatch out
of their cocoons.

Out hatched the sycamore moth.
She looked quite plain.

Out hatched the vapourer moth. He looked rather dull. He did have two white spots on his wings but they weren't very exciting.

Out hatched the puss moth. He looked fairly boring, even though his wings did have a few squiggles.

The three moths flew round the garden.

"Let's see if Woolly Bear has hatched out yet," said Sycamore.

"Good idea — at least she'll look more ordinary than us," said Vapourer.

"Look, here's her cocoon," said Puss Moth.
The three of them settled on the grass
to watch. They didn't have long to wait.

The cocoon split open,
and out hatched . . .

a lovely orange, black and white moth. She had splendid blue spots, and her body was stripy like a tiger.

"She's beautiful," said Sycamore.

"She's colourful," said Vapourer.

"She's perfect," said Puss Moth.

"And I'm not a woolly bear any more," said the newly hatched moth. "I'm a **garden tiger moth!**"

And feeling very happy she fluttered into the air.

The other three moths gazed up at her longingly.
Then all together they sang this song . . .

"Look at her!
Way up there!
No longer a small woolly bear.
She's a beautiful sight.
She's a perfect delight,
The colourful queen of the air."